COLORFUL COCKTAILS

Top 51 unusual alcoholic cocktails.

The German Kitchen

TABLE OF CONTENT

Varo Libre

Russian cola

Good morning Cuba Libre

Aurora

Sunshine

Passion fruit Mojito

Lavender Spritz

Gentle angel

Cujamara

Almond Orange

Golden lemonade

Strawberry Elderberry

Golden Copacabana

Frozen Margarita

Harvey Wallbanger

Batida de Coco

sweet punch

Poncha

Virgin Maralim

Irish Mule

Bahama Mom

Lemon Ginger Lemonade

Green Mamba Long Drink

Green sky

Grasshopper

Green Gin Cocktail

Green meadow

Tropical green

Southern Comfort

Aperol-Gin Sour

Irish colada

Ipanema Rum

Zombie

Mai Tai

Aperol injection

Arabic Sun

Raspberry - Passion Fruit - Cocktail

Vitamin gel

Italian Gipsy

Spidu

Strong Aperol

Orange Dust

Watermelon daiquiri

Cream cocktail

Advocaat with sparkling wine and grenadine

Strawberry Kiss

Tinto de Verano

Strawberry colada

Ramazzotti Rosato Duo

Strawberry Daiquiri

9 Pin Gin

Imprint

VARO LIBRE

Color of the cocktail: brown-black
Servings: 1

ingredients
15 cl grain
35 cl cola
1 lime
2 cubes
Ice

Preparation
If you like Cuba Libre or not, this cocktail always tastes good. Depending on taste, desire, and time you can choose the mixing ratio freely. Also, the cola can be exchanged.

Cut lime into pieces and take as much of it as you like. It is best to take 3 - 4 small pieces.

Place the lime pieces in a glass of an appropriate size. Then pour the grain over the lime and add the ice cubes immediately afterward. Then fill up the glass with the cola. Especially here, you can vary according to your mood.

RUSSIAN COLA

Color of the cocktail: brown-black
Servings: 1

ingredients
4 cl Gold Rum
4 cl vodka
22 cl cola
Ice

Preparation
Put a little ice in a cocktail glass. Add the rum
and vodka and top up with cola.

GOOD MORNING CUBA LIBRE

Color of the cocktail: brown-black
Servings: 1

ingredients
4 cl rum
200 ml of cola
1 dash of lemon juice

Preparation
Mix everything.

AURORA

Color of the cocktail: Colorful
Servings: 1

ingredients
250 ml orange juice
2 cl Grenadine
2 cl rum
2 cl Blue Curaçao

Preparation
Pour orange juice and rum into a glass, let the grenadine
run down a bar spoon, and finally carefully
pour Blue Curaçao onto the juice.

SUNSHINE

Color of the cocktail: Yellow
Servings: 1

ingredients
6 cl advocaat
14 cl orange lemonade
1 slice orange
Ice cube

Preparation
Pour the advocaat into a long drink glass with ice cubes and top up with Blunt or Fanta. Stir carefully and serve decorated with a slice of orange.

PASSION FRUIT MOJITO

Color of the cocktail: Yellow
Servings: 1

ingredients
6 leaves mint
1 lime
2 tsp cane sugar, brown
4 cl rum, white
1 passion fruit
Ice cube
Mineral water
Mint

Preparation
Place the mint, the lime juice, as well as 2 pieces of lime and
the cane sugar in a glass and crush with a wooden pestle.
Add the inside of the passion fruit and the rum. Add
6-8 ice cubes and top up with mineral water.
Garnish with a straw and 1-2 mint leaves.

LAVENDER SPRITZ

Color of the cocktail: Yellow
Servings: 1

ingredients
1 glass of sparkling wine
1 tablespoon lavender syrup

Preparation
Pour the lavender syrup into a champagne
glass and fill up with champagne.
Garnish with a lavender flower (meaning
a branch without green).

GENTLE ANGEL

Color of the cocktail: Yellow
Servings: 1

ingredients
1 part sparkling wine, semi-dry
3 parts orange juice without pulp
1 part vanilla ice cream

Preparation
Half fill the cocktail glasses with champagne. Add a few spoon-
fuls of the firm vanilla ice cream and fill up with orange juice.

The sparkling wine should always be poured into the glass
first so that it does not make bubbles so much. The ice cream
should not be so creamy. Otherwise, it melts too quickly.

CUJAMARA

Color of the cocktail: Yellow
Servings: 1

ingredients
0,2-liter passion fruit juice
80 ml brandy (grain)
80 ml of cream
1,5 tablespoons of sugar
½ pack vanilla sugar

Preparation
Stir everything together in a large jug until the sugar has dissolved. It tastes even better chilled, of course.

ALMOND ORANGE

Color of the cocktail: Yellow
Servings: 1

ingredients
4 cl vodka
2 cl Triple Sec
8 cl orange juice
4 cl lemon juice
2 cl almond syrup
Ice cube

Preparation
Shake everything in the shaker well.
Serve in a long drink glass with ice.

GOLDEN LEMONADE

Color of the cocktail: Yellow
Servings: 1

ingredients
4 cl brandy
160 ml lemonade

Preparation
Pour the ingredients into a glass.

STRAWBERRY ELDERBERRY

Color of the cocktail: Yellow
Servings: 1

ingredients
20 elderflower stars
5 strawberries
1 dash of lemon juice
1 shot of sugar syrup
200 ml sparkling wine

Preparation
Clean the strawberries. Cut them into slices or quarters and put them in a glass. Add lemon juice and sugar syrup. Fill up with sparkling wine. Sprinkle on elderflower stars.

GOLDEN COPACABANA

Color of the cocktail: Yellow
Servings: 1

ingredients
4 cl Batida de Coco
2 cl cachaça
6 cl Passion fruit nectar
6 cl banana nectar
Ice cube

Preparation
Prepare a long drink glass and add some ice cubes.
Fill a shaker half full with ice cubes, add all ingredients. Close and shake vigorously. Pour into the long drink glass.

FROZEN MARGARITA

Color of the cocktail: Yellow
Servings: 4

ingredients
8 cl tequila
8 cl Triple Sec
8 cl lime juice
8 cl lemonade
Ice cube

Preparation
Place all ingredients in a blender jug, mix well,
and pour into cocktail bowls. If required, decorate
with slices of lime and serve.

HARVEY WALLBANGER

Color of the cocktail: Yellow
Servings: 1

ingredients
4 cl vodka
2 cl herb liqueur
10 cl orange juice
1 slice orange

Preparation
Pour vodka and orange juice into a long drink glass filled with ice cubes and stir briefly. Add Galliano, now no longer mix. Put the orange slice on the edge of the glass.

BATIDA DE COCO

Color of the cocktail: Yellow
Servings: 1

ingredients
3 cl cachaça
4 cl pineapple juice
1 cl cream
2 cl Batida de Coco

Preparation
Prepare ingredients in an electric mixer on crushed
ice. Pour into a long drink glass filled with ice.

SWEET PUNCH

Color of the cocktail: Yellow
Servings: 1

ingredients
4 cl rum, brown
6 cl passion fruit juice
6 cl ginger ale
2 cl water
Ice cube

Preparation
Pour everything into a glass and add the ice. You can vary the sweetness depending on how much water you add.

PONCHA

Color of the cocktail: Yellow
Servings: 1

ingredients
2 cl orange juice
1 cl lemon juice
2 cl honey
2 cl cachaça
Lemon juice
Sugar

Preparation
Dip the rim of the glass in lemon juice and then in the sugar.
Put all the ingredients into the glass and stir vigorously
until the honey has dissolved. In Madeira, the stirring is
done in a large vessel with a unique, wooden stick.

VIRGIN MARALIM

Color of the cocktail: Yellow
Servings: 1

ingredients
Ice cube
2 cl passion fruit syrup
3 cl vodka
½ Passion fruit
½ Lime
100 ml apple juice
20 ml of water

Preparation
Cut a slice from half of the washed lime and cut the rest into fingertip-sized pieces. Fill a cocktail glass 3/4 full with ice and moisten it with the passion fruit syrup. Sprinkle the passion fruit and the lime pieces on top and fill up with the apple juice and water until just under the rim. Finally stir the cocktail and make it pretty with the slice of lime.

IRISH MULE

Color of the cocktail: Yellow
Servings: 1

ingredients
Ice cube
50 ml of whiskey
17 ml of lime juice
17 ml lime syrup
200 ml ginger ale
1 lime slices

Preparation
Fill a large long drink glass with ice, add whiskey, juice,
syrup, half-filled and ginger ale and garnish with a slice of lime.

BAHAMA MOM

Color of the cocktail: Yellow-Beige
Servings: 1

ingredients
15 ml of coconut rum
15 ml rum, brown
15 ml coffee liqueur
15 ml rum, white
Ice cube
Pineapple juice
1 piece of pineapple

Preparation
Put Malibu, Kahlua, brown and white rum in a shaker
and shake vigorously. Pour into a long drink glass
half filled with crushed ice. Fill up with pineapple
juice. Garnish with a thin slice of pineapple.

LEMON GINGER LEMONADE

Color of the cocktail: yellow-green
Servings: 4

ingredients
80 g sugar, brown
45 g ginger root
8 cl rum, white
1 large lemon
1 liter of water
Water, carbonated

Preparation
Put the brown sugar into a blender jug and work it into icing sugar with a few turns. Cut the ginger and lemon (complete with peel) into large cubes and add both to the sugar in the blender. Puree until a thick paste is formed. Then add the still water and mix again vigorously. Then pour into a bottle through a fine sieve. Put in a cool place.

Pour the chilled lemonade and rum into a glass and top up with sparkling mineral water as desired. If necessary, add a few ice cubes and lemon slices.

GREEN MAMBA LONG DRINK

Color of the cocktail: Green
Servings: 1

ingredients
2 cl lemon juice
10 cl passion fruit juice
4 cl liqueur 43
2 cl Blue Curaçao
2 cl cream
1 mint leaf
Ice cube

Preparation
Shake all ingredients well with 6-8 ice cubes in a shaker.
Strain into a long drink glass on a few ice cubes. Garnish
with a mint leaf.

GREEN SKY

Color of the cocktail: Green
Servings: 2

ingredients
6 cl Triple Sec
5 cl vodka
4 cl Blue Curaçao
1 orange
1 lime
200 ml tonic water
Ice cube

Preparation
Squeeze the orange and lime, pour the juice with Triple Sec, Blue
Curacao, vodka, and 3 ice cubes into a shaker and shake well.

Fill 2 long drink glasses up to half with ice cubes
and tonic water. Pour the canceled shaker contents
over the back of a spoon to form a layer.

GRASSHOPPER

Color of the cocktail: Green
Servings: 1

ingredients
2 cl cream
2 cl chocolate liqueur, brown
2 cl peppermint liqueur, green
Ice cube

Preparation
Shake the ingredients well on several ice cubes in
a shaker, pour into the glass, and enjoy.

GREEN GIN COCKTAIL

Color of the cocktail: Green
Servings: 1

ingredients
6 cl gin
2 cl lemon juice
2 cl sugar syrup
3 slices of cucumber
1 sprig of mint
1 shot of apple juice
Ice cube

Preparation
Place the gin with the ice cubes, lemon juice, sugar syrup,
cucumber slices, and mint in a shaker and shake vigorously.
Pour through a sieve into a glass with fresh ice cubes and
add a dash of apple juice (until the glass is full).

GREEN MEADOW

Color of the cocktail: Green
Servings: 1

ingredients
4 cl Blue Curaçao
4 cl vodka
16 cl orange juice
Ice cube

Preparation
First, pour Curacao into the glass, fill up with the orange juice. Add ice cubes as desired.

TROPICAL GREEN

Color of the cocktail: Green
Servings: 1

ingredients
2 cl Batida de Coco
2 cl Blue Curaçao
10 cl pineapple juice

Preparation
Just mix everything with a little crushed ice.,

SOUTHERN COMFORT

Color of the cocktail: green-blue
Servings: 1

ingredients
50 ml liqueur, Southern Comfort
50 ml of lemon juice
100 ml of cola
Ice cube

Preparation
First, mix lemon juice with the Southern Comfort.
Pour this into a long drink glass and top it up with
cola. A few ice cubes in and that's it.

APEROL-GIN SOUR

Color of the cocktail: Orange
Servings: 1

ingredients
4 cl Aperol
4 cl gin
2 cl lemon juice
2 teaspoons sugar
4 ice cubes

Preparation
Put all ingredients into a whiskey cup and stir.

IRISH COLADA

Color of the cocktail: Orange
Servings: 1

ingredients
4 cl cream liqueur
2 cl coconut rum
1 cl Grenadine
½ cl lime juice
10 cl pineapple juice

Preparation
Mix in a household blender and serve on ice.

IPANEMA RUM

Color of the cocktail: Orange
Servings: 1

ingredients
½ Lime
2 cl white rum
2 tablespoons cane sugar
60 ml passion fruit juice
60 ml ginger ale
Ice cube

Preparation
Cut half the lime into four pieces and put it into
the glass, sprinkle the cane sugar over it, and
crush it thoroughly with the pestle.

Add the passion fruit juice, rum, for and ginger ale and stir
the mixture with a straw to dissolve the limes and sugar.
Then fill a good portion of ice cubes into the glass.

ZOMBIE

Color of the cocktail: Orange
Servings: 1

ingredients
2 cl rum, white
2 cl rum, brown
1 cl apricot brandy
5 cl pineapple juice
2 cl lime juice
2 cl rum, 75%
1 slice orange
1 sprig of mint
1 cocktail cherry

Preparation
Shake ingredients except the 75% rum in a shaker with
ice and fill into the long drink glass with ice cubes.
Put the decoration on the sticker over the
glass, put mint in the glass.
Add 75% rum to the glass before serving.

MAI TAI

Color of the cocktail: Orange
Servings: 1

ingredients
4 cl rum, white
2 cl Amaretto
2 cl Triple Sec
2 cl rum, brown
100 ml of orange juice
100 ml pineapple juice
Grenadine
Ice cube

Preparation
Shake alcohol and juices with ice in a shaker vigorously, pour
into a long drink glass, with ice cubes, pour - carefully dribble
some grenadine on the ice cubes - put an orange slice and a
cocktail cherry on a sticker and serve with a long straw.

APEROL INJECTION

Color of the cocktail: Orange
Servings: 1

ingredients
4 cl Aperol
2 cl lemon juice
2 cl orange juice
Sparkling wine
Sparkling mineral water
Ice cube
Orange

Preparation
Put the ice cubes into a large cocktail or red wine glass.
Pour Aperol, lemon, and orange juice on the ice cubes.

Then fill up the glass with champagne. If you don't like
it quite so strong, you can also mix mineral water and
sparkling wine in equal parts. Serve with a straw.

ARABIC SUN

Color of the cocktail: Orange
Servings: 1

ingredients
15 cl orange juice
5 cl Triple Sec
1 cl pomegranate syrup
1 slice orange

Preparation
Fill a regular glass (not a flat glass) with Triple Sec and orange juice, then add the pomegranate syrup. Leave to stand for a few minutes so that the syrup can settle at the bottom. Garnish with an orange slice.

RASPBERRY - PASSION FRUIT - COCKTAIL

Color of the cocktail: Orange
Servings: 1

ingredients
100 ml passion fruit juice
2 cl rum
20 ml raspberry syrup
50 ml of milk
1 orange slice
Ice cube

Preparation
Put all ingredients together with some ice
in a shaker and shake vigorously.
Put some ice cubes in a long drink glass and pour the cocktail
over it. Decorate with a slice of orange and serve immediately.

VITAMIN GEL

Color of the cocktail: Orange
Servings: 1

ingredients
150 ml multivitamin juice
2 scoops of vanilla ice cream
50 ml sparkling wine
1 shot of raspberry syrup
1 orange slice
Water
Sugar

Preparation
Melt 1 scoop of vanilla ice cream into sauce. Place glass with the upper rim in water and then in sugar so that a sugar rim is formed. Then add 150 ml of multivitamin juice to the glass, then pour the champagne on top. Pour the vanilla sauce over the sparkling wine. Do not stir! Carefully add the second scoop of vanilla ice cream to the cocktail. Now put an orange slice on the rim of the glass.

ITALIAN GIPSY

Color of the cocktail: Orange
Servings: 1

ingredients
4 cl Aperol
4 cl orange juice
Champagne, dry, ice-cold
2 ice cubes
1 strawberry,

Preparation
Place two ice cubes in a stem glass. Pour the Aperol and juice
over them. Top up with champagne and stir gently.

Make a slight lateral incision in the strawberry
and stick it to the edge of the glass.

SPIDU

Color of the cocktail: Orange
Servings: 1

ingredients
50 cl sparkling wine
50 cl lemonade
1 ice cube
1 mint leaf

Preparation
Put the sparkling wine and juice, well chilled in a champagne glass and serve with an ice cube and a mint leaf.

STRONG APEROL

Color of the cocktail: Orange
Servings: 1

ingredients
1 cl Amaretto
2 cl Aperol
1 cl brandy
1 shot of orange juice
150 ml sparkling wine
Ice cube

Preparation
Pour the ingredients into a long drink glass, top up with sparkling
wine or mineral water, and serve with ice cubes if necessary.

ORANGE DUST

Color of the cocktail: Orange-brown
Servings: 1

ingredients
6 cl gin
6 cl hazelnut liqueur
12 cl coffee, cold brewed
1 orange slice
n. B.Tonic Water
Ice cube
possibly.coffee beans

Preparation
Cut a large slice from an orange. Pour half of it into a 0.5 l glass and squeeze it gently. Then add some ice cubes. Add the gin, liqueur and coffee and fill the glass with tonic water.

With the second orange slice, spread half of it once around the edge of the glass and then stick it to the glass as decoration. If you want to make the drink a little less sweet, you can add some coffee beans also fresh.

WATERMELON DAIQUIRI

Color of the cocktail: Pink
Servings: 4

ingredients
500 g watermelon, diced
10 cl rum, brown
2 tablespoons sugar, brown
6 cl lime juice or lemon juice
6 cl Triple Sec
Ice cubes or ice cubes

Preparation
Mix all ingredients in a blender to a smooth cocktail.
Divide into 4 glasses.

Of course, it also tastes good with fresh watermelon, but then the cocktail is more liquid and doesn't stay cool as long.

Quick and easy to prepare and a sweet summer cocktail.

CREAM COCKTAIL

Color of the cocktail: Pink
Servings: 4

ingredients
200 ml vodka
200 ml cream
250 ml raspberry syrup
250 ml vanilla yogurt
Ice cube

Preparation
Place all ingredients in a container and mix well.
Refrigerate and serve with ice cubes and drinking straw.

ADVOCAAT WITH SPARKLING WINE AND GRENADINE

Color of the cocktail: Pink
Servings: 1

ingredients
4 cl advocaat
2 cl Grenadine
Sparkling wine
2 ice cubes

Preparation
Put ice cubes into a glass and fill it halfway with a well-chilled sparkling wine. Stir in the advocaat and grenadine and then top up with sparkling wine.

STRAWBERRY KISS

Color of the cocktail: Pink-Orange
Servings: 1

ingredients
6 cl pineapple juice
10 cl orange juice
1 cl cream
50 ml sparkling wine
2 cl strawberry syrup
1 slice of lime
1 strawberry

Preparation
Shake the ingredients with 5-6 ice cubes in a shaker and strain into a long drink glass. Decorate with a slice of lime and strawberry.

TINTO DE VERANO

Color of the cocktail: Pink-Red
Servings: 1

ingredients
100 ml wine, rosé
200 ml lemonade
1 lime
1 lemon
Ice cube

Preparation
Gaseosa is a Spanish, slightly sweetened mineral water
with a lemon taste. Alternatively, you could make your
own Gaseosa from mineral water, with the juice of a lemon
and a little sugar, or use a slightly sweetened lemon soda.
Depending on how authentic you want it to be.

Place rosé wine and Gaseosa in the refrigerator hours before preparation and make ice cubes. Pour the ice cubes into a large glass.
Mix the cooled rosé wine in a ratio of 1:2 with cooled Gaseosa.
Cut the lime into slices and halve each slice. Put one slice of
lime into each glass. Add a dash of lemon juice. The result is a
refreshing summer drink that is very popular among Spaniards.

STRAWBERRY COLADA

Color of the cocktail: Pink-red
Servings: 2

ingredients
6 cl rum
10 cl pineapple juice
2 cl lemon juice
2 cl strawberry syrup
5 cl Cream of Coconut
Strawberries
Crushed ice

Preparation
Half fill a long drink glass with crushed ice. Mix all ingredients and some strawberries with the electric mixer, pour into the glass, and stir.

RAMAZZOTTI ROSATO DUO

Color of the cocktail: Rosé-Pink
Servings: 1

ingredients
5 cl liqueur (Ramazotti)
10 cl tonic water
Slices of lime
Ice cube

Preparation
Place the slices of lime in a wine glass and lightly toast.
Pour in Ramazzotti Aperitivo Rosato and Tonic Water
and add the ice cubes. Serve the aperitif with straw.

STRAWBERRY DAIQUIRI

Color of the cocktail: red
Servings: 1

ingredients
2 cl lime juice
5 cl rum, white
1 ½ Tbsp cane sugar, brown
6 strawberries
4 ice cubes
1 sprig of mint

Preparation
Place all ingredients in a blender and mix until
a homogenous drink is obtained.

Decorate with fresh mint.

9 PIN GIN

Color of the cocktail: red
Servings: 1

ingredients
4 cl gin
4 cl Lime Juice Cordial
2 cl lemon juice
2 cl currant syrup
4 ice cubes
10 cl mineral water
1 slice of lemon

Preparation
Put all ingredients into a glass of approx. 250 ml, stir, ready.

By adding mineral water, the taste can be individually modified and adapted.

For the non-alcoholic version, simply leave out the gin. Then it becomes the 9 pins free.

IMPRINT

The German Kitchen
Theaterstraße 8
37073 Göttingen

and

Mindful Publishing
by
TTENTION Inc.
Wilmington - DE19806
Trolley Square 20c

Instagram: mindful_publishing
Contact: mindful.publishing@web.de

Printed in Great Britain
by Amazon